For Patrick Jehle —J.W.

For Mom —P.O.

Text copyright © 2019 by Jonah Winter
Jacket art and interior illustrations copyright © 2019 by Pete Oswald
All rights reserved. Published in the United States by Schwartz & Wade Books,
an imprint of Random House Children's Books, a division of Penguin Random House LLC, New York.
Schwartz & Wade Books and the colophon are trademarks of Penguin Random House LLC.
Visit us on the Web! rhcbooks.com
Educators and librarians, for a variety of teaching tools, visit us at RHTeachersLibrarians.com

Library of Congress Cataloging-in-Publication Data
Names: Winter, Jonah, author. | Oswald, Pete, illustrator.
Title: The sad little fact / by Jonah Winter; illustrated by Pete Oswald.
Description: First edition. | New York: Schwartz & Wade Books, [2019] |Summary: "Follow a sad little fact who is locked away
for telling the truth. In its underground prison, it meets other facts, all hidden away because they could not lie. Finally, with the
help of a few skillful fact-finders, the facts are set free"—Provided by publisher.
Identifiers: LCCN 2017044465 (print) | LCCN 2017056324 (ebook) | ISBN 978-0-525-58181-9 (ebook)
ISBN 978-0-525-58179-6 (hardcover) | ISBN 978-0-525-58180-2 (library binding)
Subjects: | CYAC: Facts (Philosophy)—Fiction. | Truth—Fiction.
Classification: LCC PZ7.W75477 (ebook) | LCC PZ7.W75477 Sad 2019 (print) | DDC [E]—dc23

The text of this book is set in 24-point Brandon Grotesque.
The illustrations were rendered digitally using gouache watercolor textures.

MANUFACTURED IN CHINA
10 9 8 7 6 5 4 3 2 1
First Edition
Random House Children's Books supports the First Amendment and celebrates the right to read.

THE SAD LITTLE
FACT

written by **JONAH WINTER**   illustrated by **PETE OSWALD**

schwartz & wade books · new york

There was once a fact.

A little fact.

A sad little fact.

Then they'd walk right past it
or step over it
without so much as a blink.

The sad little fact just had one thing to say back:

A fact is a fact.

Which shouldn't have been such a big deal.

But it was.

One day, the Authorities demanded
that the sad little fact admit
that it was not a fact.
But the sad little fact could not tell a lie.
So it refused.

Now the Authorities grew angry,
and they hurled the sad little fact
into a big box, closed the lid,
and buried it deep underground.

And that was that.

Inside, the sad little fact saw that it was surrounded by other facts.
They all introduced themselves.

Christopher Columbus did not discover America.

Human beings are members of the ape family.

Dinosaurs became extinct 66 million years ago.

And so on and so forth.
It was a powerful collection of facts.

But in time, the facts grew restless.
They tired of being in a box
and wanted to get out.

I think a hole needs to be made,
suggested the sad little fact.

But—how? The facts had no tools.

Meanwhile, a bunch of lies created
by the Authorities
were taking over the world outside the box.
They too called themselves "facts,"
but they weren't.

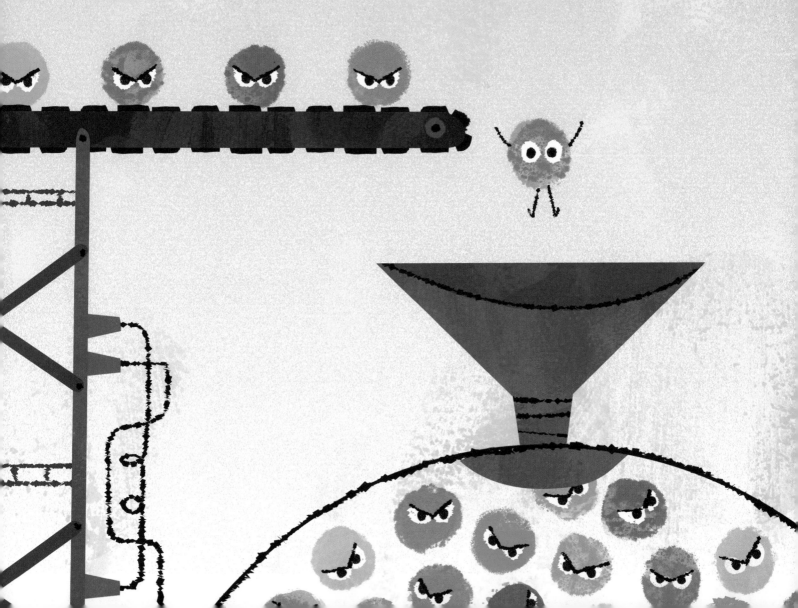

The world grew dark.

A hardy band of fact finders were
troubled by the situation.
"Where are the real facts?" they cried.
"Where have you buried them?"

But the only reply
they got was
"These ARE the facts."

And so the fact finders started digging.
Equipped with only shovels, flashlights,
and a need to know the truth,
they dug a tunnel deep, deep underground.

At last they heard voices—
the sound of facts hoping to be discovered—

They hoisted it out of the darkness
and let out the facts.

In the clear blue light of day,
the facts were glorious in all their factual splendor.

The Earth revolves around the sun!

And people are causing the Earth to get warmer!

A fact is a fact! cried the sad little fact, who was not so sad anymore.

"A FACT IS

A FACT!"

they all cried out in unison.

Some people chose to ignore the facts,
turning their backs and walking away in a huff.

But for those with minds to think
and a need to know the truth,
the facts could not be denied.

And that's a fact.